D1104030

GRAPHIC WARFARE

IWO JIMA

Graphic Planet
An Imprint of Magic Wagon
abdopublishing.com

ABDOPUBLISHING.COM

Published by Magic Wagon, a division of ABDO, PO Box 398166, Minneapolis, Minnesota 55439. Copyright © 2016 by Abdo Consulting Group, Inc. International copyrights reserved in all countries. No part of this book may be reproduced in any form without written permission from the publisher. Graphic Planet™ is a trademark and logo of Magic Wagon.

Printed in the United States of America, North Mankato, Minnesota.
102015
012016

Written by Joeming Dunn
Illustrated by Ben Dunn
Coloring and retouching by Robby Bevard
Lettered by Doug Dlin
Cover art by Ben Dunn
Interior layout and design by Antarctic Press
Cover design by Candice Keimig

Library of Congress Cataloging-in-Publication Data

Dunn, Joeming W.
Iwo Jima / by Joeming Dunn ; illustrated by Ben Dunn.
pages cm -- (Graphic warfare)
ISBN 978-1-61641-982-0
1. Iwo Jima, Battle of, Japan, 1945--Comic books, strips, etc.--Juvenile literature. 2. Graphic novels. I. Dunn, Ben, illustrator. II. Title.
D767.99.I9D86 2015
940.54'252--dc23
2015023942

TABLE OF CONTENTS

FOREWORD 4

CHAPTER 1
Surprise Attack 5

CHAPTER 2
Leading to War 6

CHAPTER 3
War 7

CHAPTER 4
In the Hands of the Allies 10

CHAPTER 5
An Island Chosen 12

CHAPTER 6
Japanese Defense 14

CHAPTER 7
Attack Plan 17

CHAPTER 8
The Invasion Begins 18

CHAPTER 9
To the Top of Suribachi 22

CHAPTER 10
The Tide Turns 24

Map 26

Timeline 28

Biographies 29

Quick Stats 30

Glossary 31

Websites 31

Index 32

FOREWORD

In the years prior to World War II, Japan was interested in territorial expansion. The country's leaders wanted to be the dominant power in the Pacific. When Germany defeated France and the Netherlands, these countries' holdings in the South Pacific were up for grabs. These islands had natural resources that were necessary for the economic self-sufficiency Japan would need to control the region.

Japanese forces devised a plan. The plan had two parts. The first was a surprise attack on the US Pacific Fleet that was stationed at Pearl Harbor, Hawaii. The second was to form a line of defense by capturing important islands such as the Philippines, Formosa, Indochina, the Dutch East Indies, Guam, and the Gilbert and Mariana Islands. Japanese officials thought if they could hold this perimeter, they could achieve their goal.

The Japanese enjoyed early success. But the US struck a fatal blow in the Battle of Midway. The Japanese lost not only four aircraft carriers, but also a cruiser, 270 aircraft, most of its best-trained pilots, and 3,500 men. With its naval strength lessened, Japan scaled back its expansion plans. However, the Japanese would not give up.

Slowly the Allies retook strategically important territory. The Allies wanted to use the B-29 Superfortress to attack the Japanese mainland. To do so, they needed an airstrip on the east side of the country in order for Tokyo to be within the plane's range. Just 750 miles (1,207 km) south of Tokyo lay Iwo Jima. Its three airstrips would be valuable additions in the war against Japan. On February 19, 1945, the battle for possession of the island began.

1 SURPRISE ATTACK

2 LEADING TO WAR

3 WAR

JAPAN, GERMANY, AND ITALY SIGNED THE TRIPARTITE PACT ON SEPTEMBER 27, 1940, AS A PROMISE TO PROTECT ONE ANOTHER. TOGETHER, THEY BECAME THE AXIS POWERS.

THE JAPANESE MILITARY HAD SUCCESS EARLY ON.
BANZAI!

THEY HAD COMPLETE NAVAL AND AIR SUPERIORITY, EVEN DEFEATING THE POWERFUL BRITISH NAVY.

BY THE EARLY PART OF 1942, THE JAPANESE EMPIRE CONTROLLED SIGNIFICANT PARTS OF ASIA.

ALASKA (USA)
CANAD
USSR
MONGOLIA
MANCHURIA
Japanese Empire
KOREA
JAPAN
CHINA
OKINAWA
MARIANA ISLANDS
FORMOSA
IWO JIMA
HAWAII
BURMA
SIAM
PHILIPPINES
FRENCH INDOCHINA
Pacific Ocean
GUAM
MARSHALL ISLANDS
PAULA ISLAND
CAROLINE ISLANDS
TARAWA
DUTCH EAST INDIES
NEW GUINEA
SOLOMON ISLANDS
GILBERT ISLANDS
GUADALCANAL

JAPAN WAS WELL AWARE OF THE INDUSTRIAL MIGHT OF THE UNITED STATES.
ADMIRAL YAMAMOTO ISOROKU ORGANIZED THE ATTACK ON PEARL HARBOR.
HE REALIZED JAPAN'S BEST HOPE FOR VICTORY WAS TO DESTROY THE US PACIFIC FLEET.
WE HAVE AWAKENED A SLEEPING GIANT.
39
THE TURNING POINT OF THE WAR WAS THE BATTLE OF MIDWAY IN JUNE 1942.
THE JAPANESE NAVY LOST FOUR OF ITS AIRCRAFT CARRIERS.

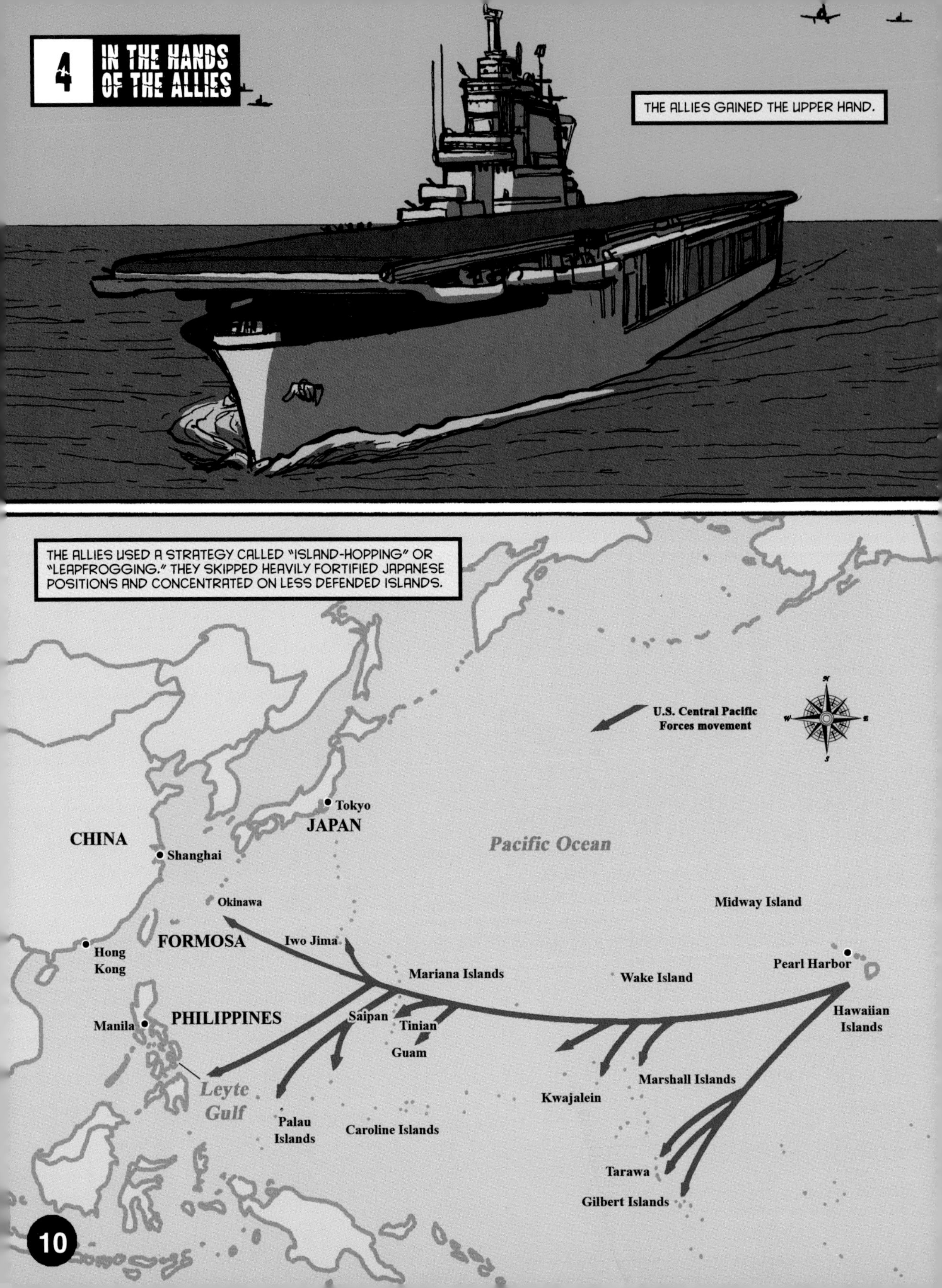
4
IN THE HANDS OF THE ALLIES
THE ALLIES GAINED THE UPPER HAND.
THE ALLIES USED A STRATEGY CALLED "ISLAND-HOPPING" OR "LEAPFROGGING." THEY SKIPPED HEAVILY FORTIFIED JAPANESE POSITIONS AND CONCENTRATED ON LESS DEFENDED ISLANDS.
U.S. Central Pacific Forces movement
Tokyo
JAPAN
CHINA
Shanghai
Pacific Ocean
Okinawa
Midway Island
FORMOSA
Iwo Jima
Hong Kong
Mariana Islands
Wake Island
Pearl Harbor
Manila
PHILIPPINES
Saipan
Tinian
Guam
Hawaiian Islands
Leyte Gulf
Palau Islands
Caroline Islands
Kwajalein
Marshall Islands
Tarawa
Gilbert Islands

THE JAPANESE MILITARY WAS FURTHER PRESSED WITH LOSSES IN GUADALCANAL AND NEW GUINEA.
LET'S GO, BOYS!
HIT 'EM WHERE IT HURTS!
AMERICAN SUBMARINES PATROLLED JAPANESE SHIPPING LANES.
FIRE TORPEDO!

IN LATE 1944, ALLIED FORCES AND FILIPINO GUERRILLAS HELPED FREE THE PHILIPPINES.
AND, THEY DESTROYED MANY OF JAPAN'S SUPPLY LINES.

5 AN ISLAND CHOSEN

IWO JIMA WAS JUST 750 MILES (1,207 KM) SOUTH OF TOKYO, JAPAN, AND IT CONTAINED THREE AIRFIELDS.
JAPAN
Tokyo
Pacific Ocean
IWO JIMA
MARIANA ISLANDS (U S)
Saipan
Tinian
Guam

THE ALLIES COULD USE THE AIRFIELDS AS A STAGING AND REPAIR AREA.

AND THEY COULD ALSO ELIMINATE THE POSITION ON THE ISLAND'S MOUNT SURIBACHI FROM WHICH THE JAPANESE WERE SHOOTING AT ALLIED PLANES.

6
JAPANESE DEFENSE
LIEUTENANT GENERAL KURIBAYASHI TADAMICHI WAS ASSIGNED THE TASK OF DEFENDING IWO JIMA.

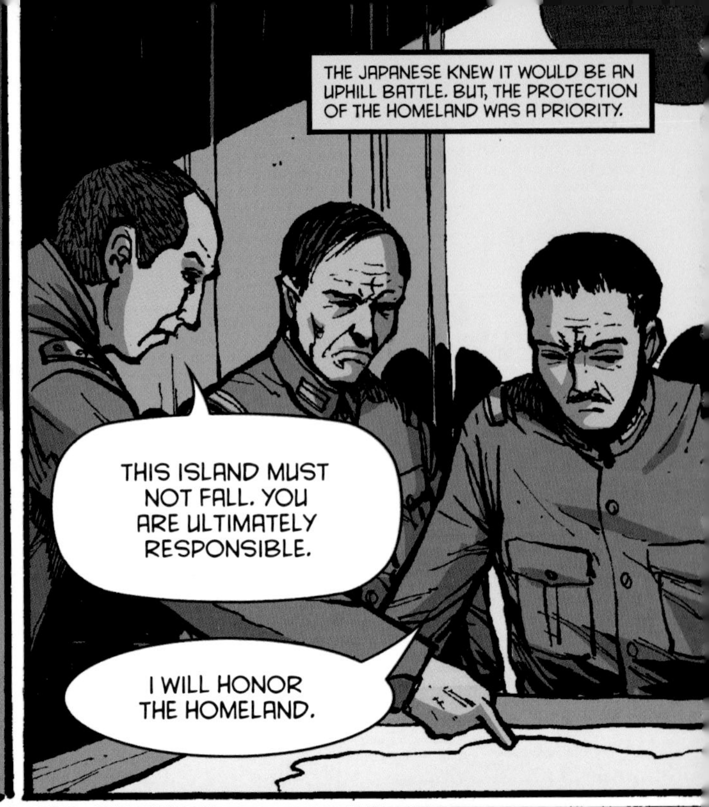
THE JAPANESE KNEW IT WOULD BE AN UPHILL BATTLE. BUT, THE PROTECTION OF THE HOMELAND WAS A PRIORITY.
THIS ISLAND MUST NOT FALL. YOU ARE ULTIMATELY RESPONSIBLE.
I WILL HONOR THE HOMELAND.

KURIBAYASHI'S RESOURCES WERE LIMITED.

HE HAD APPROXIMATELY 20,000 TROOPS, WITH SUPPORTING ARTILLERY AND TANKS.

THE NORMAL JAPANESE DEFENSE METHOD WAS TO STOP BEACH LANDINGS. KURIBAYASHI DECIDED NOT TO FOLLOW THIS METHOD.
I THINK IT WOULD BE FUTILE TO TRY TO STOP ANY LANDING.
WHAT ARE YOU THINKING?

WE SHOULD REINFORCE OUR POSITION ALONG THE MOUNTAINS OF THE ISLAND.

THEY BUILT PILLBOXES DEEP INTO THE ROCKS OF IWO JIMA. THE VOLCANIC ASH OF THE ISLAND WAS EASILY CONVERTED INTO CONCRETE.

CAMOUFLAGED ARTILLERY UNITS WERE SCATTERED ABOUT FOR SUPPORT.

KURIBAYASHI KNEW HIS TANKS WOULD BE EXPOSED. SO, HE BURIED THEM TO ALLOW FOR THE GREATEST PROTECTION.
THE MAIN PART OF THE DEFENSE WAS A SERIES OF UNDERGROUND TUNNELS.
THESE TUNNELS WERE USED TO INTERCONNECT THE KEY DEFENSIVE POSITIONS.

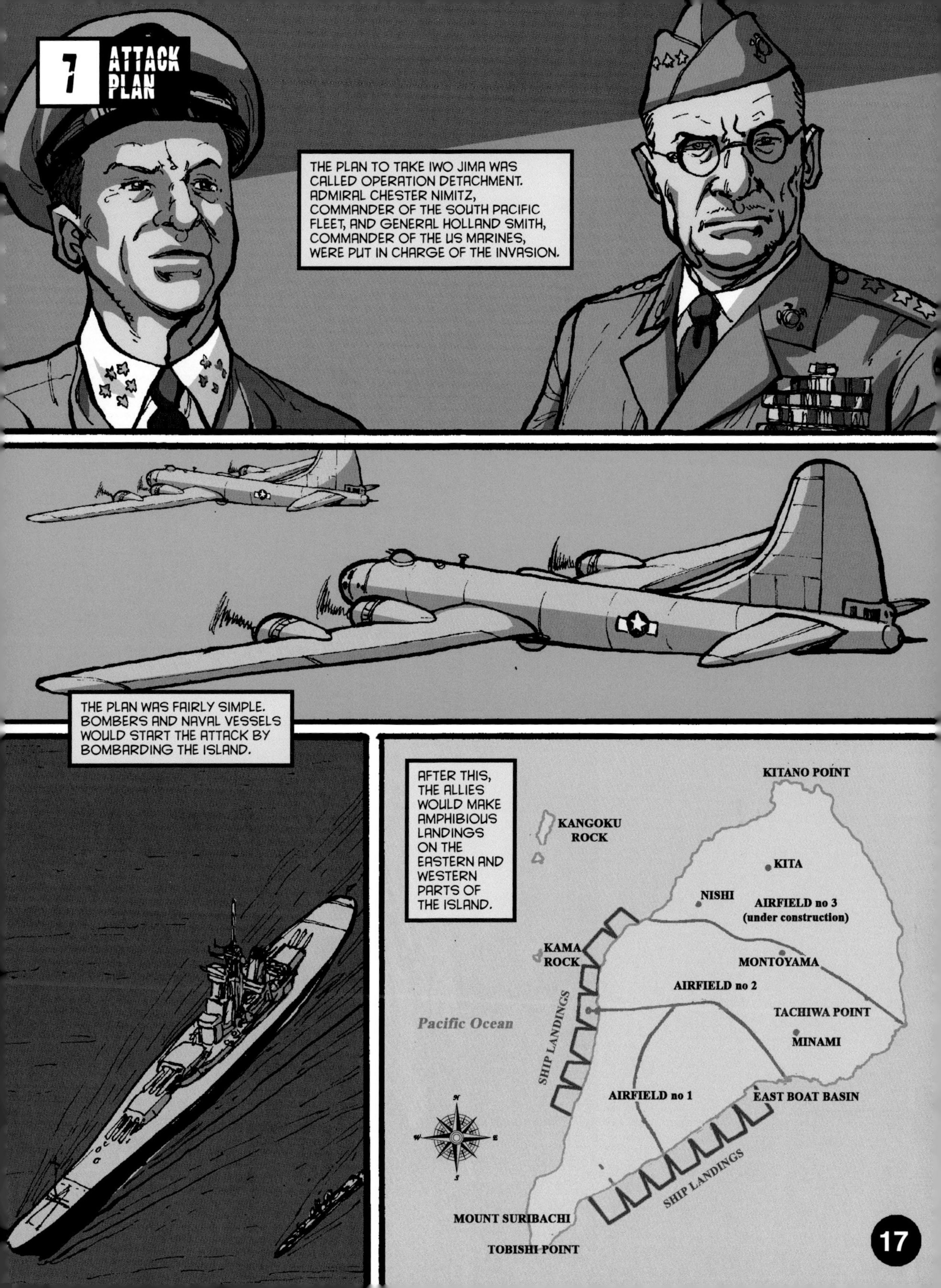
7
ATTACK PLAN
THE PLAN TO TAKE IWO JIMA WAS CALLED OPERATION DETACHMENT. ADMIRAL CHESTER NIMITZ, COMMANDER OF THE SOUTH PACIFIC FLEET, AND GENERAL HOLLAND SMITH, COMMANDER OF THE US MARINES, WERE PUT IN CHARGE OF THE INVASION.
THE PLAN WAS FAIRLY SIMPLE. BOMBERS AND NAVAL VESSELS WOULD START THE ATTACK BY BOMBARDING THE ISLAND.
AFTER THIS, THE ALLIES WOULD MAKE AMPHIBIOUS LANDINGS ON THE EASTERN AND WESTERN PARTS OF THE ISLAND.
KITANO POINT
KANGOKU ROCK
KITA
NISHI
AIRFIELD no 3 (under construction)
KAMA ROCK
MONTOYAMA
AIRFIELD no 2
SHIP LANDINGS
TACHIWA POINT
Pacific Ocean
MINAMI
AIRFIELD no 1
EAST BOAT BASIN
N
W
E
S
SHIP LANDINGS
MOUNT SURIBACHI
TOBISHI POINT

8 THE INVASION BEGINS

THE FOURTH AND FIFTH MARINE DIVISIONS BEGAN THEIR LANDING ON IWO JIMA ON FEBRUARY 19, 1945.
HEADS UP, FELLOWS! HERE COMES THE BEACH!
WATCH FOR SNIPERS!
WHEN THE MARINES ARRIVED ON THE BEACH, THERE WAS VERY LITTLE RESISTANCE.
WELL, THIS WAS EASY.
LOOKS LIKE OUR PLANES AND NAVY BOYS GOT 'EM ALL.
NOW?
PATIENCE . . .
WHAT THEY DIDN'T REALIZE WAS THAT THE JAPANESE WERE HIDDEN AND READY TO ATTACK. THEY WERE WAITING FOR MORE MARINES TO ARRIVE SO THEY COULD HURT THE MOST SOLDIERS ALL AT ONCE.

MORE MARINES MOVED INLAND.
OKAY . . . LET'S CLEAR OUT THIS PLACE.
FIRE!
SOON, THE MARINES WERE UNDER HEAVY FIRE FROM PILLBOXES AND ARTILLERY BEHIND REINFORCED STEEL DOORS.
THE JAPANESE HAD PLACED THEIR PILLBOXES TO COVER THE MOST AREA.
NORTHERN SECTOR
RESERVE AREA MOTOYAMA
EASTERN SECTOR
WESTERN SECTOR
SOUTHERN SECTOR
MOUNT SURIBACHI SECTOR
MAIN CROSS-ISLAND DEFENSES
SECONDARY LINE OF DEFENSES
PRIMARY ARTILLERY

THE ASH OF THE ISLAND MADE IT DIFFICULT FOR THE MARINES TO DIG FOXHOLES FOR PROTECTION.
I CAN'T STACK UP ANY OF THIS STUFF!

THE MARINES SLOWLY BEGAN MAKING PROGRESS ON THEIR ATTACK.

BUT, THE JAPANESE HAD BUILT A COMPLEX TUNNEL. THIS AIDED IN THEIR DEFENSE.

AS THE MARINES PASSED BY PILLBOXES AND BUNKERS THEY THOUGHT THEY HAD DESTROYED, THE JAPANESE USED THE TUNNEL SYSTEM TO TAKE BACK THE BUNKERS.

9 TO THE TOP OF SURIBACHI

US NAVY CORPSMAN JOE ROSENTHAL WITNESSED AND PHOTOGRAPHED THE RAISING OF THE SECOND FLAG.
IRA HAYES, FRANKLIN SOUSLEY, MICHAEL STRANK, JOHN BRADLEY, RENE GAGNON, AND HARLON BLOCK RAISED THE SECOND FLAG.
THE PHOTO WAS SENT TO THE ASSOCIATED PRESS IN NEW YORK AND WAS SOON PICKED UP BY US NEWSPAPERS. IT BECAME ONE OF THE ICONIC PHOTOS OF WORLD WAR II AND WAS USED TO HELP SELL WAR BONDS.

10 THE TIDE TURNS

THE JAPANESE EMPIRE SURRENDERED ON AUGUST 15, 1945, AFTER THE ATOMIC BOMBS WERE DROPPED ON HIROSHIMA AND NAGASAKI. ON SEPTEMBER 2, SURRENDER DOCUMENTS WERE SIGNED ON BOARD THE USS *MISSOURI*.

THE MEDAL OF HONOR IS THE HIGHEST MILITARY AWARD. TWENTY-SEVEN MEDALS WERE AWARDED TO THOSE WHO WENT ABOVE AND BEYOND THE CALL OF DUTY DURING THE BATTLE OF IWO JIMA.

ON THE TOP OF MOUNT SURIBACHI, A MEMORIAL STANDS ON THE EXACT SPOT WHERE HAYES, SOUSLEY, STRANK, BRADLEY, GAGNON, AND BLOCK RAISED THE FLAG.

ROSENTHAL RECEIVED THE PULITZER PRIZE FOR HIS ICONIC PHOTO.
THE IMAGE WAS LATER USED AS A MODEL FOR THE US MARINE CORPS WAR MEMORIAL IN ARLINGTON, VIRGINIA.

MAP

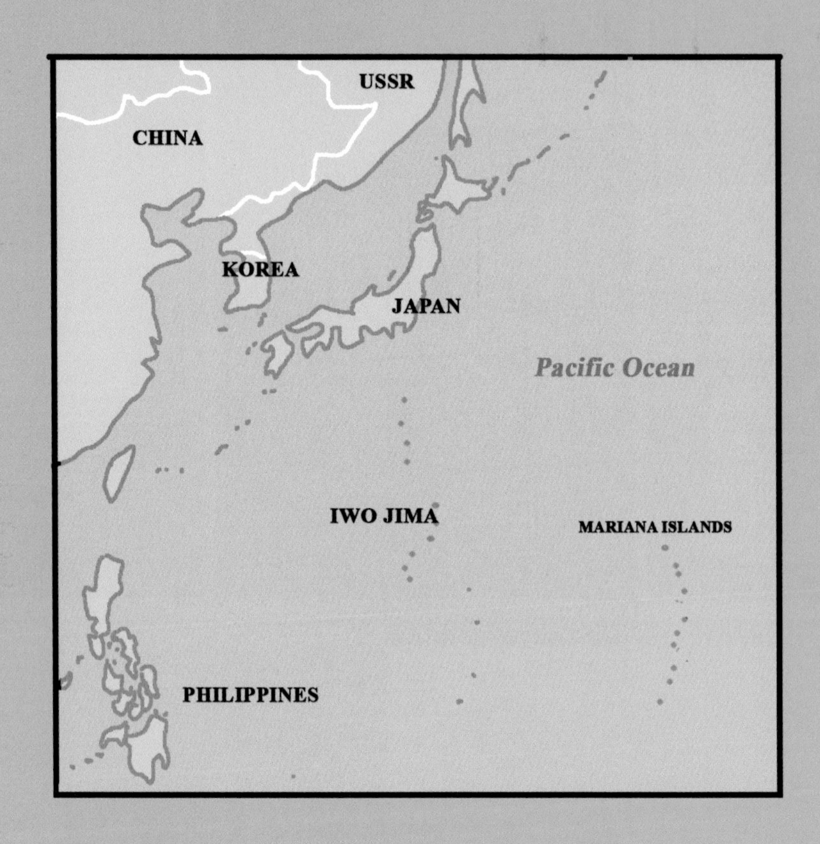

Japanese Defense Lines

MARINE ADVANCEMENTS

5th Division

4th Division

3rd Divisions

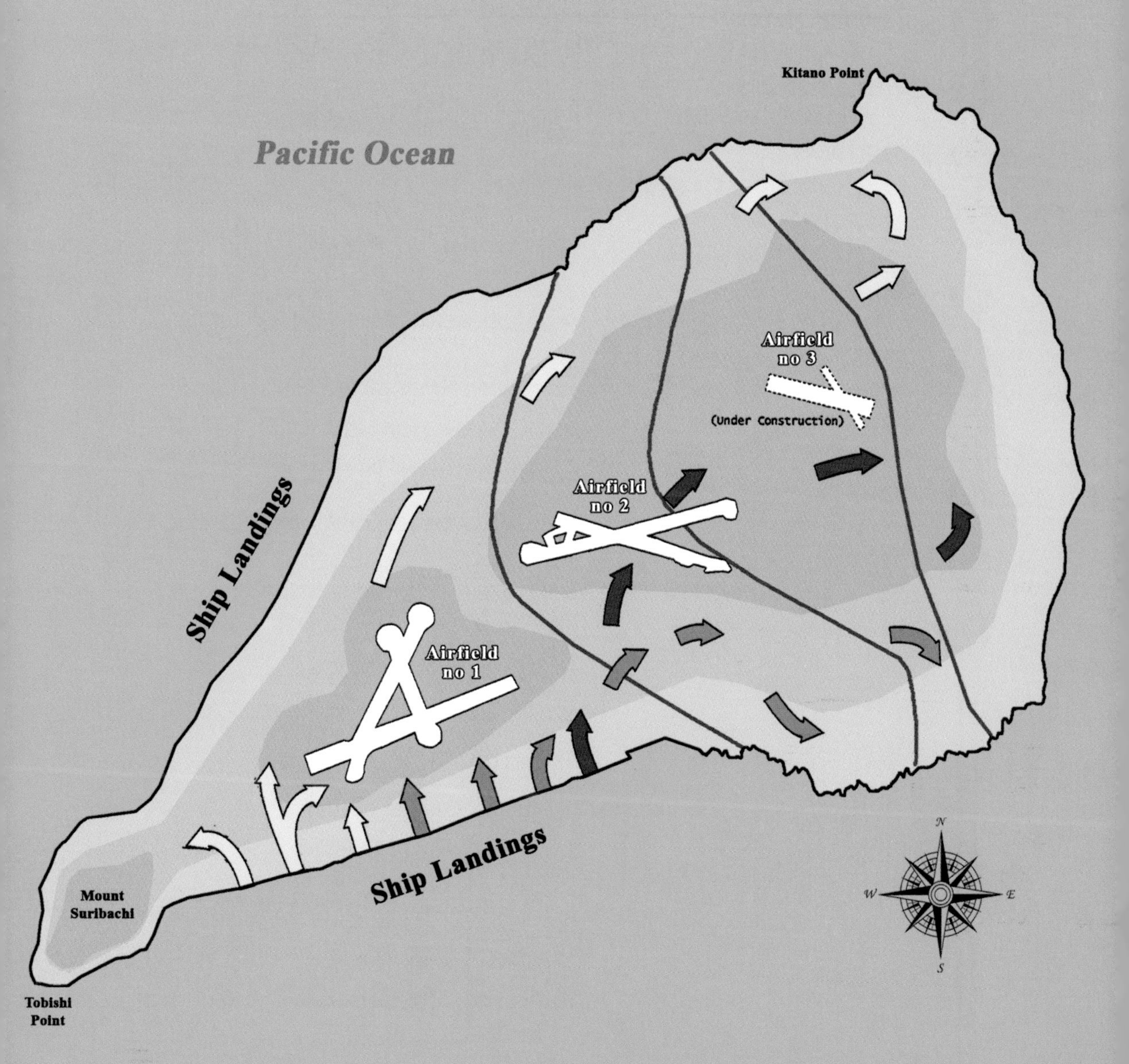

Kitano Point
Pacific Ocean
Airfield
no 3
(Under Construction)
Airfield
no 2
Airfield
no 1
Ship Landings
Ship Landings
Mount
Suribachi
Tobishi
Point
N
W
E
S

TIMELINE

1940 September 27
Japan, Germany, and Italy signed the Tripartite Pact.

1941 December 7
Japanese attacked the US Pacific Fleet at Pearl Harbor, Hawaii.

1941 December 8
Japanese attacked US bases in the Philippines.

1942 May 6
Japan secured the Philippines.

1942 June 3-7
Japan and the US fought the Battle of Midway.

1944 June 15
The US began bombing Japanese defenses on Iwo Jima.

1945 February 16
The US fired upon Iwo Jima for three days.

1945 February 19
US Marines invaded Iwo Jima.

1945 February 23
Five marines raised the US flag on top of Mount Suribachi.

1945 March 26
US Marines defeated Japan and secured Iwo Jima.

1945 August 15
Japan surrendered, ending World War II.

BIOGRAPHIES

KURIBAYASHI TADAMICHI

(July 7, 1891–March 6, 1945)

General Kuribayashi Tadamichi was leader of the Japanese forces during the Battle of Iwo Jima. Kuribayashi was born in 1891 in Nagano, Japan. After graduating high school, he joined the Imperial Japanese Army. From March 1928 to May 1930, he lived in the US, where he toured the country and attended Harvard University. During the Battle of Iwo Jima, he commanded more than 20,000 soldiers. Nearly all of them died there, including Kuribayashi. His body was never found.

CHESTER NIMITZ

(February 24, 1885–February 20, 1966)

Admiral Chester W. Nimitz was commander of the US Navy's Pacific Fleet during World War II. Nimitz graduated from the United States Naval Academy in Annapolis, Maryland, in 1905. In World War I, he was chief of staff to the commander of the Atlantic submarine forces. During World War II, he took command of the Pacific Fleet after the Japanese attack on Pearl Harbor, Hawaii, in 1941. In 1942, he won the Battle of Midway. He won battles in the Solomon and Marshall Islands and the Philippines among others. In 1944, Nimitz was promoted to Fleet Admiral, the navy's highest rank. On September 2, 1945, Nimitz signed the Japanese Instrument of Surrender for the United States. He died on February 20, 1966, at California's Yerba Buena Island.

QUICK STATS

World War II

Dates: 1939–1945

Number of Casualties:

For the Allies:
126,753,851

For the Axis powers:
12,461,741

Belligerents:

The Allies:
Russia, British Commonwealth, United States

The Axis powers:
Germany, Japan, Italy

Important Leaders:

For the Allies:
US president Franklin D. Roosevelt, British prime minister Winston Churchill, Soviet Union leader Joseph Stalin, US general Dwight D. Eisenhower

For the Axis powers:
German chancellor Adolf Hitler, German field marshal Erwin Rommel, Japanese emperor Hirohito, Japanese prime minister Hideki Tojo, Italian prime minister Benito Mussolini

GLOSSARY

allies
people, groups, or nations united for some special purpose.

armada
a group of warships.

artillery
large guns that are used to shoot over a great distance.

atomic bomb
an extremely powerful bomb that uses the energy of atoms.

banzai
a determined, often reckless attack by Japanese soldiers in World War II.

barrage
a line of weapon fire used to stop an enemy and protect one's own soldiers.

bond
a certificate sold by a government. The certificate promises payment of a certain amount on or before a given future date.

bunker
a shelter dug into the ground to keep people safe from attack.

economic
relating to the production and use of goods and services.

fortify
to strengthen against attack, especially by providing walls, ditches, or forts.

futile
having no result or effect.

guerilla
a member of a band of fighters. Guerrillas are not usually part of a regular army. They fight their enemies with sudden and surprise attacks.

infamy
being famous or well known for bad or evil things.

pillbox
a small, low structure for machine guns and antitank weapons.

Pulitzer Prize
one of several annual awards established by journalist Joseph Pulitzer. The awards honor accomplishments in journalism, literature, drama, and music.

secure
free from risk of loss.

significant
large enough to be noticed or to have an effect.

sniper
a soldier who shoots at individuals from a hidden place.

strategic
relating to a plan that is created to achieve a goal.

strategy
the planning of military operations.

suicide
the act of taking one's own life.

WEBSITES

To learn more about Graphic Warfare, visit booklinks.abdopublishing.com. These links are routinely monitored and updated to provide the most current information available.

INDEX

A

Allied powers 4, 10, 12, 13, 17, 18, 24

Arizona 5

Asia 8

Axis powers 7

B

Block, Harlon 23, 25

Bradley, John 23, 25

C

China 6

D

Dutch East Indies 4

F

France 4

G

Gagnon, Rene 23, 25

Germany 4, 7

Gilbert Islands 4

Guadalcanal 11

Guam 4

H

Hayes, Ira 23, 25

Hiroshima, Japan 25

I

Italy 7

Iwo Jima 4, 12, 13, 14, 15, 17, 18, 19, 24

J

Japan 4, 5, 6, 7, 9, 11

K

Kuribayashi Tadamichi 14, 15, 16

M

Manchuria 6

Mariana Islands 4

Midway, Battle of 4, 9

Missouri 25

N

Nagasaki, Japan 25

Netherlands 4

New Guinea 11

Nimitz, Chester 17

P

Pearl Harbor, Hawaii 4, 5, 9

Philippines 4, 8, 11

R

Rosenthal, Joe 23, 25

S

Schrier, Harold 22

Smith, Holland 17

Sousley, Franklin 23, 25

Strank, Michael 23, 25

Suribachi, Mount 13, 22, 24, 25

T

Taiwan 6

Tokyo, Japan 4, 13

Tripartite Pact 7

U

US Marine Corps War Memorial 25

US Pacific Fleet 4, 9

Y

Yamamoto Isoroku 9